GLACIERS

GLACIERS

a novel

by Alexis M. Smith

For Wren

Amsterdam

Isabel often thinks of Amsterdam, though she has never been there, and probably never will go.

As a child in Soldotna, on Cook Inlet in Alaska, she saw volcanoes erupting, whales migrating, and icebergs looming at sea before she ever saw a skyscraper or what could properly be called *architecture*. She was nine years old, on a trip to her aunt's with her mother and sister, the first time she visited a real metropolis: Seattle. She took it all in—the towering buildings and industrial warehouses, the train tracks and bridges, the sidewalk cafés and neighborhood shops, and the skyline along Highway 99, the way the city seemed to rise right up out of Elliot Bay, mirroring the Olympic Mountains across the sound. The breadth and the details overwhelmed her, but soon she loved the city in the same way she loved the landscape of the north. Old churches were grand and solemn, just like glaciers, and dilapidated houses filled her with the same sense of sadness as a stand of leafless winter trees.

Soon after her trip to Seattle, she began collecting postcards of other cities: Paris, London, Prague, Budapest, Cairo, Barcelona. She borrowed books from the library and watched old movies, just to get a glimpse of these other places. She imagined visiting them, walking the streets, sleeping in creaky beds in hostels, learning a few words of every language.

Postcards

Isabel finds the postcard of Amsterdam on Thursday evening, at her favorite junk store, across from the food carts on Hawthorne. It is a photograph of tall houses on a canal, each painted a different color, pressed together and tilted slightly, like a line of people, arm in arm, peering tentatively into the water. The picture has a Technicolor glow, the colors hovering over the scene rather than inhabiting it.

Isabel turns the postcard over, expecting nothing—an antique white space never utilized—like others on the rack, bought decades ago on

long-forgotten vacations, and never mailed. But
Amsterdam had been stamped; Amsterdam had
been posted. The postmark is dated *14 Sept 1965*
and there is a message, carefully inscribed:

Dear L—

*Fell asleep in a park. Started to rain. Woke up with
my hat full of leaves. You are all I see when I open
or close a book.*

Yours,

M

Isabel stands before the rotating metal rack
for a long time, holding the postcard, rereading the
message, imagining the young man (it must have
been a young man) whose small, precise hand-
writing stretches across allotted space perfectly.
She imagines the young woman (Miss L. Bertram
2580 N. Ivanhoe St. Portland, Ore) who received

the postcard, and how much she must have read between those few lines, how much she must have longed for him to say more.

Isabel turns back to the image of Amsterdam, wondering if the houses on the canal still stand, or if they have succumbed to time and damp. Amsterdam is one of those low-lying cities, she thinks, remembering a *New Yorker* article about melting icecaps.

She searches the rack for more of Amsterdam and the correspondence between M and L, but finds none. She buys the postcard and leaves with it tucked deep in her coat pocket.

Walking home, she thinks Amsterdam must be a lot like Portland. A slick fog of a city in the winter, drenched in itself. In the spring and summer: leafy, undulating green, humming with bicycles, breeze-borne seeds whirling by like tiny white galaxies. And in the early glorious days of fall, she thinks, looking around her, chill mist in the mornings, bright sunshine and a halos of gold and amber for every tree.

Back in her apartment she pins Amsterdam to the wall above her bed, beneath another old postcard: four brightly painted totem poles and a few muskeg spruce, leaning over a marshy inlet.

Glaciers

Isabel's parents returned to Alaska soon after she was born. They had lived in Washington for four years, since Isabel's older sister, Agnes, was born. First they lived in a dumpy apartment over a drugstore in Bellingham, then in a cooperative household in Seattle, with three other families, several cats, and a blind Labrador retriever named Little John. Isabel's father was a musician, who had dropped out of music school. He worked odd jobs and gave the occasional guitar lesson. Isabel's mother stayed home with Agnes, cooking and gardening with the other women in the household.

With one child the family might have gone on like this. Isabel was born on Valentine's Day, 1979, and within a month her parents decided to go back to where they had grown up, where her father could get a good-paying job on the North Slope.

Isabel doesn't actually remember, but she imagines the voyage now, twenty-eight years later.

The ferry from Seattle was crowded with other families, not Alaskan families but the kind of loose-minded travelers who pointed and photographed without really seeing.

Like other great creatures before them, the glaciers were dying, and their death, so distant and unimaginable, was a spectacle not to be missed. The ferry slowed where a massive glacier met the ocean; a long, low cracking announced the rupture of ice from glacier; then came the slow lunge of the ice into the sea. This is *calving*—when part of a glacier breaks free and becomes an iceberg—a kind of birth. The calving sent waves, rocking the ferry. Hands gripped railings and feet separated on gridded steel. There were shouts of appreciation and fear, but nothing like grief, not even ordinary sadness.

North of Juneau, the boat lingered near some rocks. A voice announced that below, starboard, was the wreck of the Princess Sophia, sunk in a storm just before the Armistice. A gale whipped the ship over some rocks and tore her open like a can of salmon. All aboard died in the oily, frigid water. Only the captain's wolfhound, who made the dark, impossible swim to shore, survived. He shivered and howled along the rocks until rescuers carried him away. Only a few yards of mast were visible above water, and the wind and waves had driven the bodies of passengers and crew miles along the coastline.

The travelers, pondering this tragedy, lined the rails to peer into the water. Somewhere beneath them, they contemplated, were the disintegrating remains of a boat not so different from the one they were on. What did they expect to see in that water? Their own wavering reflections stared gravely back at them.

Isabel's family sat in the commissary during the viewing of the Princess Sophia, eating sandwiches with no lettuce.

Only a few grainy photographs actually remain to tell the tale. In the first, she is dressed in hand-knit blue wool. The smallest living thing, even smaller than the gulls. Her father holds her, his back against the railing, her mother and Agnes to the left. Behind them: deep dark water and stony sky. The porpoises that sometimes surfaced are not surfacing. The whales that sometimes arched smoothly over the waves, are not worrying the water's fractal plaintiveness. Other photographs are notable for what is absent: her mother, who was the photographer, only appears at the beginning of this story, for the family portrait, then disappears.

The steaming boat eventually harbored. There were long hours on land in a car, north, then south again, down the peninsula to Soldotna, named (some said) after the Russian word *soldat* for soldier. A small city on the Kenai River known for its salmon and halibut fishing, and as a gas and bathroom break on the way to Homer.

Outside town was the homestead of her father's grandmother, Agnes, her sister's namesake, who had died the previous summer. Three rooms with a wood stove and running well water. A small garden with raspberries and a weedy patch of Sitka strawberries. An acre of woods. Her mother made the beds with felted-wool and down blankets. The cast-iron pans and chipped china came with the house. Her father hung a rope swing for her sister from the tallest tree. Her mother started seeds in the greenhouse. The aspen and birch were just opening up, shuddering off the cold.

Secondhand

She wakes just before her alarm goes off, stretches her arm over the pillows and cat to reach the clock. The crows woke her, in the trees outside; they had slipped into that place between dreaming and waking. The crows in the trees outside her window flew into the thrift shop. A whole murder of them landing on the hanging clothes, making a racket in the fluttering dresses. Her recurring dream: finding a small vintage shop set in the side of a decaying building; rows and rows of old clothes to get lost in. She was trying on the perfect blue wool coat, a Pendleton or maybe a London Fog, perfect for walking in the fall, by the tall houses on an

Amsterdam street. Then the crows; then the coat disappears and she feels the dream escaping, tries to conjure it back. Crows. She burrows her head under the pillows, stretches her warm legs into the cool, vacant places in the sheets.

There's no use resisting the morning now; she's awake. Cat nudging her shoulder. Garbage truck outside accompanying the crows. Isabel scratches the cat's whiskers and rubs her head with her palm.

You're such a good cat, she says. And then she says it again, *such a good cat*, because she tends to say things twice to animals.

She sits up, throwing her legs over the edge of the bed, and the cat jumps down, underfoot all the way to the kitchen. The early morning sunlight warms a patch of linoleum and she lets her feet bathe in it while the kettle heats on the stove.

I think I'll buy a new dress for the party tonight, she tells the cat. A new dress, she says, thinking of her dream, and all the other times she's had the dream, and how odd it is to dream again and again of thrift stores.

In some of the dreams, the store is run by knowledgeable older ladies who were in the theater in their younger lives. In others, she finds herself in junk stores and church shops, where she finds a stash of coats and dresses, all the former property of some meticulous, stylish dame who passed away with several decades' worth of fashion archived in her closets. In many of these dreams, Isabel becomes disoriented, or suddenly loses her glasses and can't see, or she realizes she doesn't have any money and she has to leave it all behind. Or sometimes, as she's trying on a dress, feeling the satin lining slip over her skin, she falls into a narcotic sleep—a dream of sleep—and wakes up—actually wakes up—in her bed, with her striped sheets and the cat licking herself, and the crows outside, and the garbage trucks.

What a symbol, she thinks, to have running around your head.

But there it was, every so often, making her want things. The way she hungered for things when she woke! Secretary blouses, chinois bathrobes, houndstooth skirts, Pendelton jackets. She has a closet full of old clothes, still she dreams about them.

She looks around her kitchen at the accumulation of years' worth of seeking out church rummage sales and small town junk shops: the mismatched teacups and saucers in the cupboard, the faded aprons hanging from hooks on the door, the Vera tea towels in a basket on her tiny kitchen table, between the rooster and hen salt and pepper shakers.

In her old apartment, in the top floor of a ninety-year-old house, these things do not look out of place, but as she gazes at them Isabel realizes that these things were all new, once. They were purchased and carried home in boxes or department store shopping bags. Perhaps they were given as gifts. Their value was their newness, once, and none of these things would have gone together in a kitchen of any decade before now. A new bride would have wanted a set of matching china, complete with serving platters and gravy boats. The rooster and hen of the 1940's would have looked hopelessly old-fashioned next to the bright, geometric-print linens of the 1960's. The hand-sewn aprons would have been folded away in a drawer or hung on the back of the door, not displayed as if they were objects to be admired.

But Isabel does admire these things. She feels a need to care for them that goes beyond an enduring aesthetic appreciation. She loves them like adopted children.

She butters a piece of toast, pours a cup of tea and spoons some honey. Her mother had a way of stirring honey into tea—counterclockwise four times, then clockwise once—that Isabel has practiced since she was a little girl. There was something in the angle of her mother's wrist, and the calm, distant gaze out the kitchen window, that made her seem younger, prettier. Isabel realizes now that she had been seeing through her mother, to the woman she had been before she and Agnes were born.

She takes a bite of toast and sits at the table with her breakfast. The cat rubs herself against Isabel's bare legs. Out the window a single crow swoops and rests on the telephone line, silently. The line dips and sways. Isabel sips her tea and stares at the bird against the pale morning sky, thoughts drifting from crow, to dream, to dress, to what she will wear today (the brown skirt with the kick pleats, she thinks, and the dark blue White Stag blouse she found in Astoria last summer).

The crow drops from the line, sails away.

Afterlife

She was four, not yet in school, when her father first took her junking. It began with biscuits and gravy at the High Tide Diner in Old Kenai, a few blocks of nearly dilapidated clapboard buildings with pitted and rocky parking lots overlooking the delta of the Kenai River and Cook Inlet. The waitresses, whose regulars were leathery from cigarettes and the sea, or missing fingers from the canneries, fussed over the young father and his plump, blue-eyed little girl who liked to stand inside the vinyl booth and look back into the room through the mirrors along the walls. (What she saw: the backs of old men smoking at the counter; the soda fountain; the waitresses sorting flatware and pouring coffee; the little window where the plates of food came out of the kitchen; and the most peculiar thing, on the wall above the cash register, a photograph of Mt. Redoubt varnished to an enormous piece of driftwood, with hands that ticked around an invisible clock.)

After breakfast they climbed back into her father's rusty orange Chevy pick-up and took an unpaved back road to the Salvation Army Thrift Store. Isabel's father flipped through bins of records and she wandered around, looking for treasures.

There are treasures everywhere, her father told her.

What kind of treasures? she asked.

All kinds. Like this, he said, grinning, holding up a record with a picture of a woman covered from head to toe in whipped cream.

Oh, Isabel said, unsure if this was actually proof.

Belly, he said, putting the record down on his stack and squatting down next to her, it's a treasure if you love it. It doesn't matter how much it costs, or whether anyone else wants it. If you love it, you will *treasure* it, does that make sense?

Yes, she said, though it was still unclear. She loved biscuits and gravy. She loved watching snow fall. She loved to swing so high her toes seemed to brush the tops of the trees.

Her father went back to the records and Isabel looked around her. They were the only customers in the store. An elderly woman hobbled from the back with an armload of scarves. Isabel set off in the opposite direction, passing racks of men's clothes, shelves of pots and pans, bins of weathered sports equipment.

Along the way she stopped, pointed to objects and turned back to her father asking, Daddy, do I love this hat? Do I love this jar? Daddy, do I love this snowshoe?

I don't know, Belly, do you? her father replied, every time.

Eventually she lost sight of him and continued to wander through the store. She climbed onto a stool by the cash register, where there was a glass case full of jewelry and knick-knacks. She peered through the glass at the pendants and rings and ceramic figures—a pair of cats, a sheepherdess, an elaborately decorated woman's shoe that would fit into Isabel's palm.

Then she noticed a shoe box on top of the counter full of old photographs. Most of them were black and white, some of them on stiff cardboard with names and dates she couldn't read written on the backs. She picked up one, then another, looking carefully at the people, especially their expressions and clothes. She took in the whole box with her small fingers and serious gaze. There were children with buttoned boots and unsmiling fixed faces. Young women in lacy dresses, holding bouquets of flowers, colors faded. Family portraits in front of houses and cars, and one with a horse. There were entire families there, dispossessed, thrown together like refugees.

They must be lonely, she thought, and scared, all night in the cold, quiet shop.

She carefully sorted through them until she found the few she must save. Among them: two little blonde girls, probably sisters, posed in matching dresses with big bows and lace-up boots; a young man in a military uniform, in front of a white farmhouse; and a sad-looking young woman in a pale flowered dress and sunhat, sitting in the tall grass by the sea.

What did you find, Belly? her father asked her, when he found her.

These people, she said, holding out her pictures, fanning them a little, like playing cards.

Those are pretty old, aren't they? he said, looking them over. He looked up at her. Well, now you know what treasures are, he told her.

She took them home and asked for a special box to put them in. Her mother found an orange pekoe tin in the back of the kitchen cupboard and tapped the tea dust from it over the sink.

For years Isabel kept the tin of pictures in her sock and underwear drawer, taking them out every now and then when she was alone. She invented stories for them, based mostly on bits of other stories she gleaned from her grandmother's cribbage friends.

One of the sisters died, at nineteen, of the Spanish flu. The other grew up to be the girl in the grass by the sea, who was the young soldier's sweetheart. The soldier lost his mind in the trenches; his sweetheart never married. She sold fabric and notions in the general store and kept the bundle of her soldier's letters in her delicates drawer next to a ring box containing a lock of her sister's hair.

She carried the photographs with her from year to year and from house to house, after her parents' divorce, when she was ten, and then again, when she was eleven, and their mother moved to New Mexico with the man she met in a photography class, her father moved with the girls to Portland. The people in the photographs came to mean as much to her as her own relatives. She had rescued them in her Alaska, her home, and carried them with her into a new life in the city. She imagined them looking in on her from the afterlife, grateful, watching over her. She would occasionally climb the maple in her yard and look up at the sky, trying to imagine a time when her own existence, her clothes and haircut, and the saturated colors of their family snapshots, would be antique. She knew that it would happen, but she could not imagine what that future might look like, or what her place might be in it. All she could do was hope she did not end up in a shoe box at a the Salvation Army Thrift Store.

City Trees

Downtown in the morning, everyone moving, the trees listing, the bricks and green speckled with pigeons and starlings. Isabel steps off the bus and onto the sidewalk. She moves more quickly than she would like, in the fresh air, drawn along by all the other moving bodies. Shoes clicking and clapping around her. Suits and leather satchels brushing past, disappearing through glass doors, into tall buildings. Trains stopping and starting. The bus pulling away from the curb with a raspy cough.

A few yellow ginkgo leaves flutter from a tree and Isabel watches them eddy around the elk statue and into the fountain below. No one else seems to notice, moving so quickly up the sidewalks.

Isabel thinks of Amsterdam. She wonders what kind of leaves fell into the young man's hat. Amsterdam, like Portland, is full of trees. Elms and planes: old giants, planted like soldiers in long rows along avenues and in city squares. Most of the trees of Amsterdam were planted after the war, when almost all of the trees and much of the city were destroyed. Isabel remembers the passage in Anne Frank's diary, about glimpses of a chestnut tree and the sky, hemmed by a small window. Anne's tree survived the war, but Isabel read in the newspaper recently that it is rotting from within, and there was talk of cutting it down.

Isabel lifts her gaze to the umbrella of leaves overhead, framed by the tall buildings. There are Dutch elms and London planetrees along with the ginkgos.

Chestnut leaves would be too big to fit into a hat, she thinks.

Isabel waits for the light, shuddering with the easterly breeze at an intersection, skirt clinging to her bare legs, skin prickling all over. She clutches her sweater to her. The people around her become rigid while the breeze weaves through them, some turning into it, some away. As the light changes, the breeze shifts the leaves and the sun warms her again. She steps off the curb into the street and hastens her pace to the library.

The Wounded

Isabel turns the metal knob on her office door and pushes until she feels the thump of the door against her chair. She glances at the cart of books in the hallway outside her door: the wounded. All day Isabel presides over the library's damaged books, which, ironically requires lots of paperwork.

But she actually loves her job. She abandoned writing for library science in college, at the urging of her grandmother, who claimed there was no market for *being in love with words*. Isabel chose her area of specialty, preservation and conservation, as a minor rebellion and as a matter of course—salvaging the mistreated came naturally to her, though it might not be the most *marketable* skill she could acquire.

She drops her bag on her desk then pulls off her sweater, hanging it over the back of her chair, and listens for sounds of habitation around her. She likes arriving early, settling in before everyone else arrives.

Up and down the hall are other small offices and meeting rooms, for others like her: the subspecialists, the techies, the genealogists, the archivists. The librarians work upstairs, in larger, brighter, carpeted rooms, with newer computers, and more comfortable chairs. This part of the basement was once a bomb shelter; her office was once a mop closet.

You work in the secret underground! her best friend, Leo, had exclaimed the first time he visited her at work.

Then he told her about the sewers in comic books—the kind inhabited by acid-drenched humans and the bitter, discarded former pets of urbanites. The hero goes there to find unlikely allies against the real evil, the great evil, the one living right out in the open, driving the fancy car and hosting cocktail parties. Monotonous and thankless as her job can be somtimes, she cheers at the thought of her coworkers—a dozen of them crammed into their little offices in the basement—all cleverly disguised as harmless geeks, all capable of saving the world if called upon to do so.

Walking down the hall she sees a shadow in the kitchenette, probably Spoke, from tech support, who arrives earlier than anyone else. The thought of him gives her insides a little stir. His given name is Thomas, but everyone calls him Spoke, even their boss. Spoke is the nickname he got in the war, and though no one here was in the war with him, it comes out naturally, as if it were the only way to acknowledge what he has been through without actually bringing up the war.

She makes her way down the hall, composing herself, the weight of a cup in her palm.

Think pretty thoughts, she tells herself, remembering something her mother used to say to her about *thinking pretty being pretty*. Her mother was full of vaguely quotable advice for life, which she collected and offered but seemed to have no further use for herself, like a linty tissue pulled from a coat pocket.

Isabel's pretty thought: autumn leaves drifting to the ground; a couple—the lovers from the postcard—under the trees.

Spoke hunches over a mason jar full of black coffee with his back to the door. A dusty blue sweater with blown out elbows, foot tapping to his own hum. It pleases her to see him like this, sitting at the little table as she enters the break room nearly every morning, his black glasses fogged with coffee steam. It is as close as she has been to waking up with him.

Good Morning, Isabel, he says without looking up. He's reading the newspaper.

Good morning, Spoke, she says.

She turns to the cupboard and waits to feel his eyes on her. Waits, and pretends to look through the box for a tea bag, though it is right there, the Earl Grey she has every morning.

There is a physics to their relationship. She feels the attraction as a force, like the gravitational tug of celestial bodies in orbit; but it seems that to touch, one of them must crash into the other.

She fills her cup with hot water from the spout on the water cooler, spoons honey and waits. She feels the hairs on the back of her neck and the ungainly reach of her limbs. She stirs, puts the hot spoon into her mouth, the metal and sweetness burning her tongue.

They have worked together for a year, since Spoke got out of the war. This fact—that he was a soldier—made them all a little nervous at first, having heard stories of trauma leaving people unhinged. Like a screen door slapping the side of a house until it finally flies off in a gale.

He was not like that. Or any of the other images Isabel might have conjured for the word *soldier*. Meat. Packaged meat. The grill of a truck. Cinder blocks. All vaguely unpleasant but ubiquitous things. All symbols for things Isabel would rather not explore in detail: the viscisitudes of war and its biproducts. But no: there was Spoke on his first day, bike helmet in one hand, offering the other to everybody in turn. Old button-down shirt and beaten jeans, rolled up at one ankle, in the cyclists' way, revealing a striped sock. Glasses slightly out of style. Everything slightly out of style, as if he had been away awhile.

Isabel was familiar with this condition, present in people who have been living abroad or off the grid. In Alaska the popular trends arrived slowly, if they ever made it at all. So that when her family moved to the States, when she was eleven, her middle school classmates thought her anachronistic—a remnant of two or three years past. This, she thinks, probably determined her taste in clothes for the rest of her life.

In a similar way, Spoke was a curiosity for everyone at the library. He had lived somewhere foreign, in circumstances they barely sketched in their minds (with disproportionate emphasis on dramatic weather). Molly, who worked across the hall, had once said that Spoke seemed not quite present. For Isabel it was more that his presence called to mind a time *before*. Before *what*? she thought. Before the war, maybe? Or more likely some in-between time, when the war existed, was taking place, but everyone thought (or hoped) it would be over swiftly. It was a time of breath-holding.

When she turns back to the table, he picks up a spoon and stirs his coffee. She leans against the counter, fingers wrapping around the cup and meeting on the other side. He taps the spoon against the glass rim. He closes his eyes and inhales coffee vapor.

Now she can't imagine a soldier unlike Spoke.

She seats herself and takes measured sips from her cup.

What's new in the world? she asks, shuffling the paper, glancing at the headlines.

They regard each other across the table.

Do you want the good news or the bad? he asks.

There's good news? she brightens.

He smiles with one half of his mouth.

He refolds the Metro page and hands it to her, and picks up the Arts. They both read. He hums a little louder, the same four bars.

She listens. They read. The sounds of paper between them as they turn and crease and carefully avoid touching each other. Then, sounds of their coworkers arriving, doors unlatching and footfalls. Their morning ending.

Time to work, she thinks. She closes her eyes and breathes all the way to the bottom of her lungs.

She wants him to want to be looking at her.

Lungs

Before Isabel could read, she loved books. They had one bookshelf in the homestead and if she were left alone too long as a baby or toddler, she would pull every book from the low wooden shelves. She remembers the weight of them heaped over her small legs, the coolness of them on her bare skin. She loved to find the pages of *The Fanny Farmer Cookbook* that had smudges of batter and saucy fingerprints, and to gaze at the Garth Williams illustrations in *Little House in the Big Woods*, from which her parents read a chapter aloud every night the winter she turned four.

She remembers sitting in an armchair with Agnes reading the nature encyclopedia, screaming over and over again, first with fright, then glee, when they turned to the magnified pictures of spiders. Her sister read that spiders have *book lungs*, which fold in and out over themselves like pages. This pleased Isabel immensely. When she learned later that humans do not also have book lungs, she was upset. Book lungs. It made complete sense to her. This way breath, this way life: through here.

Leo, her best friend since middle school, wrote his name in every book he checked out from the library the whole time he was a teenager. The first was *Giovanni's Room*. It was his form of tagging. He chose the pages carefully, to exact the most symbolic significance. Thus the small, all-caps black lettering, LEO, adjacent the gayest of passages in every book. Other books he marked: *Our Lady of the Flowers*,

Apartment In Athens, *The Good Soldier*. When he revealed his habit to Isabel and she scolded him.

Those are library books, Asshole, not men's room stalls, she said. Why don't you just lift gay books from Powell's like a normal juvenile delinquent?

A decade later, when she started working at the library, she wondered if one of Leo's books would find her. It was a shock, when one finally appeared. She had almost forgotten. It was a copy of Elizabeth Hardwick's *Sleepless Nights*. As she pulled the book from her cart it bloomed open in her two hands. With an exhausted, papery sigh the pages fell out one by one and drifted to the floor. Isabel bent down to pick up the pages and there was Leo's name, on page ninety-seven, next to a passage about "the travels of youth, the cheapness of things" and Amsterdam.

After work that day she went to a barbeque at a coworker's house. Spoke was there, too, though he was new to the library then, and when Isabel saw him sitting alone at the kitchen table, she quickly took the seat across from him. After hellos, they sat in silence watching others. A band was setting up outside under the carport. People positioned lawn chairs and laid out blankets on the scrappy patch of grass. The summer light was fading and there was a lightness in the air, so that voices seemed to float in the window several seconds after they were spoken. Someone plugged in some Christmas lights and folks let out a cheer.

Isabel and Spoke both smiled at the sound.

Then there was smalltalk. She asked how he was settling in to the job?

He talked about getting used to new people, new routines. Then he asked her about her day.

Isabel started to give a rote reply, then she remembered Leo's book. She told Spoke about the book falling apart in her hands, finding Leo's name, how improbable it was that she should find that page in that book. She had tacked it to the wall by her desk.

He asked about Leo.

We met in sixth grade homeroom, she said. She wiped the condensation from her bottle of beer as she talked.

I call him Loon. He had a high-pitched, wavering voice that the other boys made fun of. The first time I heard it, during roll call, it reminded me of the loons we used to hear on Skilak Lake in Alaska.

She took a long drink and he took a long drink and they set their bottles down at the same time.

What's your story? she asked.

My story?

You were in Iraq, right? Isn't that where you got your nickname?

He leaned back in his chair and stretched his arms behind his head and clasped his hands behind his skull. He was wearing a worn T-shirt with the image of U2's *Boy* and for a moment his pose mirrored the one of the little boy on the shirt. He looked curiously at Isabel, and she felt he was measuring her in some way. Not physically, not for prettiness; not for intelligence even. Then he put his elbows back on the table.

Well, he starts, Since we're talking about books, there *is* a book in my story.

He told her about a copy of *Dhalgren* he took with him to Iraq and kept in his vest pocket sometimes. He read a lot of science fiction, then. He had just finished *The Stars My Destination*, and someone recommended Samuel Delaney for something different. He picked *Dhalgren* because he liked the weight of it in his hands and it looked long enough to last him a while.

He paused, and seemed to be done with his story. He took another drink and looked out into the room. Isabel leaned closer. She got the feeling he was talking to her like she was a woman—or no, maybe just a naïve, liberal civilian—he was censoring himself, choosing his words deliberately, when the words that naturally came out might be profane.

Do you really want to hear this? he asked.

Only if you want to tell me, she said.

He seemed to weigh this, then nodded and sighed.

He fixed machines in Iraq. Armored vehicles and tanks, mostly, but also radios, flashlights and the personal electronic devices of his friends. He fixed everything that crossed his path—even things that didn't seem to need fixing—they all worked a little better after he'd tinkered with them. He got a reputation as *the fix-it guy*.

So when did you meet the bicycle? Isabel asked.

He looked her in the eye for a long time, wondering, she imagined, whether he should laugh and jokingly tell her to fuck off, then end the story. But he liked her, she could tell, and this made her brave enough to ask and look right back at him without demurring.

How do you know there's a bicycle? he asked.

There must be a bicycle in this story, or we'd be calling you Transmission. Or Headphones.

He smiled, shaking his head.

I'd take Headphones, he said.

She softened then, realizing how close she was to an experience she had no right to be glib about.

He took another drink.

We were outside Haditha, he said. There had just been a lot of trouble with insurgents there, but it seemed to be dying down. Where we were, near this village on the Euphrates, things were calm. We were waiting for something. Those times can be worse than being in the fray, in a strange way. You start to remember what normal is like. You see or hear something that reminds you of home—it can be anything, a dog loping along a ditch, a whistled tune, anything—and then you get this yearning. . .

That day I saw something: a couple of kids—boys, ten or twelve years old—trying to ride a busted bicycle down this pitted dirt road. It was ancient—who knows where they got it?—the frame was bent, the chain kept slipping off. It was too big for these kids and one of them crashed, just bit the dust. And just like that I was back in Wisconsin, watching the neighbor kid fall off his bike outside our house, crying over his scraped up knee, then climbing back up on the seat and pedaling home, snot running down his face.

I guess I was staring at them for a long time. I was with my sergeant and a few guys at the time.

My sergeant slapped me on the back and said: Dahl, why don't you go over there and fix that bike.

He thought it was funny. I'm always fixing shit. I walked over and gestured to the bike. The kids didn't run away—they were used to us by then— they just handed it over and stood back. I monkeyed with the chain—I didn't have tools on me, just a utility knife. My Sergeant and the other guys thought it was fucking hilarious. They were about twenty yards away, across the road, grinning and talking shit. The kids just watched over my shoulder. I finally got it fixed so the chain wouldn't slip off, so I gestured to the kids, but they wouldn't try it. They were shaking their heads like, No way, man, you first.

I thought, Fuck it. Give 'em a show. So I sat on the seat—jammed way down, knees up around my elbows—and I rode that thing around in circles in the dirt. My sergeant was shaking his head, and the guys and the kids are laughing and hooting. I looked ridiculous, I'm sure. The last thing I remember is the face of the kid who fell in the dirt—he just stopped laughing all of a sudden. A Humvee about a hundred and fifty meters or so to my left was approaching a donkey cart—(he paused, looking out into the yard as two guys hauled a cooler over to the carport)—and the donkey exploded.

What?

There was an IED on the donkey, or the cart, or maybe on some trash in the road. They put them in anything innocuous—soda cans, women—or repellent, like dead dogs. The donkey, the cart and everything in and around it blew. We were just beyond the radius of the blast—the kids, me, the bike—we all got hit.

When I woke up, there was a spoke in my rib cage.

Isabel winced.

It pierced my right lung—I landed on it, actually. I woke up long enough to know I was hurt, then passed out again. I was lucky—no head trauma, no major organs, just a few burns. One of the kids died from shrapnel, I don't know which one. I just picture the kid who fell off the bike. In my dreams sometimes he's the neighbor kid from my childhood. And sometimes he's a ten-year-old me.

He paused. Then he took a deep breath and exhaled out his mouth. He looked at her and his body relaxed, his shoulders released.

The weird thing, he said, is that the spoke hit my lung but missed the copy of *Dhalgren* in my vest pocket. It scraped past the bottom pages, left a little scar on it, but the words were untouched. I read it in the hospital. More than once.

Do you still have the book? she asked.

He nodded.

Will you ever read it again?

No.

Loon

She closes her office door, picks up the phone and calls Leo. She listens to the ringing on the line and glances over at the page from *Sleepless Nights* tacked to the wall with Leo's name etched into it. The coincidence strikes her—how Leo wrote his name, all those years ago, on the page about going to Amsterdam, and how she was thinking of Amsterdam and the lovers, now, because the postcard, at home tacked to her wall.

Bell? comes his voice.

Hi, Loon, she says, feeling suddenly incapable of communicating verbally.

I need your help, she blurts.

In trouble already? It's barely lunch, girl.

I'm on a break, she says.

Oh, he says. I see. Wolf or woodsman?

Woodsman.

The one?

The same.

Oh, Bell, he says, sighing.

I know.

Tough love or shoulder to cry on?

Let me have it, please.

Gladly, he says, clearing his throat. Men are simple, Bell. Especially swarthy young woodsmen. He wants to know that you need him. He'll stay out there in the trees toiling away till you call him to come running with his hatchet.

Won't that be a thrill, she says.

I'm a little jealous, I admit, he replies.

What fairy tale are we in, anyway?

Doesn't matter.

Of course it matters. Anyway, I was thinking of asking him to the party tonight.

Yes. Do it.

Are you bringing someone?

Mm, he hesitates. There may be a potential fellow there. —Little Red Riding Hood?

More like Little Blue Vintage Coat. —How should I ask him? Like I know it's a date, or more casual, like it's just a thing we could do, as two friendly coworkers? I hate this part. I'm so bad at this part.

Muster up your courage, march on over there and ask him like you just tromped through the thorny brambles to find him.

You're clever, but really.

Listen to me.

I listen. I'm listening.

You've been here before, Bell. Remember the stories you told me about wandering in the woods when you were a little girl? It scared the crap out of you, but you went out there all alone, knee-high to a bunny rabbit, and picked berries and climbed trees and found bird nests and came home all bug-bitten and mossy. And you loved every minute of it. It made you our beautiful Arctic Bell, impervious to cold and feared by mosquitoes. Aren't you glad you didn't stay by grandma's side, darning socks and baking gingerbread?

Who darns socks?

Girls nobody tells stories about.

Bones

She walks down the hall to the bathroom. After checking for feet under the stall doors, she goes to the mirror. She washes her hands, dirty from the books she has handled all morning. She watches the water flow over her hands and down the drain, then quickly glances up at her reflection in the mirror. It's a game she plays with herself. She thinks if she just sees herself from the right angle, when she's not thinking about it, the mirror will show her something that she has never seen before, something that other people see.

At a family party when she was about nine, she

overheard an aunt say: Isabel is a bit homely next to Aggie, isn't she?

Homely was a new word, so Isabel went to the dictionary. She never looked in the mirror the same way again.

She was plump, awkward, eyes too big for her face, hair twisted in spitty wisps. She thought she looked good in her older sister's nicest hand-me-downs—clothes that had always received compliments when Aggie wore them—but she started to see how the sleeves were too tight around her upper arms, and how the buttons of the blouses strained to stay in their holes around her tummy.

Did you eat a whale for breakfast? she remembers a scrawny boy named Derek asking her in fourth grade.

They were lining up to return to the classroom after recess. She pretended to ignore him, bracing herself for the punch line, already feeling the blood rush to her cheeks.

Because you are what you eat and you look like a beached whale, he finished.

No one thought it was funny, but no one came to her defense, either.

That night after her bath she stood in front of the mirror and stared at herself. She loved whales. Once, in Resurrection Bay, a young gray whale who lost his pod followed the boats around for several weeks. Isabel was on a tourboat with relatives from the States. They watched the whale come closer and closer to their boat until he actually bumped it lightly, rubbing against the hull lovingly, like a cat. He swam away, then back again, coming up just enough to make contact, rocking the boat like a cradle. Isabel had seen whales before, but she had never felt quite so close to one, looking into his great big black eye and seeing herself.

I'm a whale, she said into the bathroom mirror.

I'm a whale! she shouted.

Her mother knocked on the door and opened it without waiting, looking alarmed. Isabel blushed.

Everything okay, Belly? she asked.

Isabel wrapped a towel around herself. Her mother sat on the toilet behind her and their eyes met in the mirror. They looked nothing alike. Her mother was diminutive, with fine, delicate features, freckles and dark brown curly hair. Agnes took after their mother.

Isabel looked just like pictures of her father's Irish grandmother when she was a young woman, a fisherman's daughter—later a fisherman's wife—larger and heavier in bones and flesh.

If I were a whale, Isabel said, trying to avoid the question, I would be a narwhal.

She imagined spearing scrawny little Derek through the heart with a giant tooth.

Her mother smiled weakly.

Isabel, she said seriously, believe me when I tell you that everything is temporary. Everything. There's not a thing in the world that will not change, including you.

She looks at herself in the mirror now. Her light brown hair is gathered up at the back of her head in a messy bun, with wavy strands falling around her face. She pulls the pencil out of it and then lets it down. She searches her pocket for her lip gloss and leans in to apply it to her lips. She stands back to assess and relaxes the space between her eyebrows. She has thick eyelashes and blue eyes. A small dark mole marks her upper right cheek, below her eye. She plucks at her cheeks to make them fill with blood, and watches the blush spread over her skin.

Her mother was right, she admits. She grew taller, those bones and that flesh had spread out.

She practices a smile—a real smile, the one she would give Spoke if she had the courage. She thinks, for the first time, that it is possible she is actually quite beautiful, and she wishes Spoke could see her just then, the way she catches herself.

Danish Modern

As she leaves the library, there are no human sounds, only machine sounds: the refrigerator humming, the susurration of the vents, their steady, mechanical exhalations. Everyone has slipped out for lunch ahead of her.

Outside at midday, Isabel feels the last breath of summer on her skin. The hum of the library still in her ears, but drowning now in the noise of the city. She smells the food carts from blocks away, the hot oil and garlic and roasting meat that flows through the air every work day, mingling with the rank warm sewers and the burnt-oil musk of the

buses and delivery trucks, and under that, when her feet tread the grass under the trees, the smell of damp bark and vegetal decay.

She breathes it in and lets herself think of Spoke. She imagines walking with him, like this, through the city. Telling him how cold air and leaves and gasoline smell like the first day of school to her.

It's a strange product of infatuation, she thinks. To want to tell someone about mundane things. The awareness of another person suddenly sharpens your senses, so that the little things come into focus and the world seems more beautiful and complicated.

When M wrote to L, she thinks, he didn't tell her about his journey. There was no description of the city, or his lodgings or museums. The brevity of the postcard—the intense focus on the moment in the

park—it was as intimate as a young man could be. Like reaching out and brushing a strand of hair from her eyes.

Isabel imagines M and she can't help seeing him as a character in an Antonioni film: young, disaffected, wandering. He wears a wrinkled button-down shirt and a jacket, trim trousers, and of course the hat—a dashing straw fedora, brown with a dark band. She sees him clearly, though in this film of hers everything is just barely in color—like the postcard.

She thinks of everything she knows about 1965 and comes up with a meager tableau of the Vietnam War, Pucci prints and Danish Modern furniture. But M, she can see clearly. He could be the prototype of any young man in her city: the mustachioed barista, the tattooed bookseller, the plaid-shirted clerk at New Seasons Market.

This is the way it would have been for L, too, Isabel thinks: never having been to Amsterdam, she could only picture him in a city like her own. She would close her eyes and see him sitting under the trees, taking off his hat and resting it beside him, brim up. He reclines on the grass, propped on one elbow, and opens his book to her—the picture of her he keeps between the pages.

Isabel tries to picture L: a woman in her twenties, like Isabel, on the cusp of possible love, going about her life in this city, waiting for postcards. But she can't see her. She can only *feel* for her.

Choirgirl

Isabel turns down Oak toward the little vintage shop at Fourth, thinking of lunch—the Chinese place in Old Town—casting around inside herself for hunger, imagining the tastes of things.

She walks up to the stoop of the vintage shop. It looks dark—no sign on the door to indicate whether it is open or closed, or what the business hours might be. Isabel knows this already, from previous visits. Isabel peeks through the window. The mannequin in the window, dressed in something Joan Crawford could have worn—elegant but angular, all shoulders—is headless, and her fingers are chipping away. Beyond the racks of dresses and blouses and coats, sees a dressmakers dummy moving.

Traffic thrums on the street behind her. She tries the door—unlocked—and a small string of bells jangles against the glass as she pulls it open and steps inside.

Hello! comes the muffled voice of the shop-keeper, and she pops up from behind the counter, bright white hair piled on to of her head. She lifts her hand in greeting, a pin cushion attached at the wrist.

Hi, Isabel waves.

Oh, hello! she recognizes Isabel now. It's Nancy Drew, isn't it?

Good memory, Isabel says. The woman helped her assemble a girl sleuth costume last Halloween.

And how did it go?

Perfect, she answers, her hands already running through the dresses on the rack to her right.

Of course it was, the woman answers, amused, turning back to her mending. Isabel remembers this amusement from the last visit, as well. The woman seems ready to be pleased with the world.

Isabel looks around and quietly inhales. She loves the smell of old things. Every available space bursts with clothing. Open hat boxes full of hankies, taffeta-lined suitcases offering slips and garters, circles within circles of shoes atop the racks scrunched with skirts and blouses. For a moment she is back in this morning's dream, amid the clothes, smelling the decay of cloth and leaves, feeling the weight of sleep in her limbs and waiting for the birds to crow.

She moves among the clothes, eyes drifting up to the dresses suspended from the ceiling, hovering far above her head, swaying, as if dancing. She wonders what a group of dresses would be called, if they were living things: *a choir*, she thinks, *a choir of dresses*.

So, what brings you in today, hon?

Isabel looks back at the shopkeeper, unsure of how to answer.

A party dress, she says finally.

Ah-ha! the shopkeeper says, pleased. What kind of party dress?

Blue? she says, apologetically, shrugging.

The shopkeeper laughs, a strand of white hair falling into her face.

Well, she says, I've worked with less. How about this: what kind of party?

It's for a playwright who just won some prestigious award. It's at his loft, in Old Town, a renovated casket factory.

Ah, I know the place, the lady says. Will there be dancing?

Probably.

Definitely, I would say.

She sticks a needle in the pin cushion and pulls it from her wrist. She walks over to Isabel and stands back to take a look at her.

You're about, what? Twenty-nine inch waist?

Isabel nods.

I may have something in back—from an estate sale last month. I'll have to dig for a minute. Meanwhile, you look around—you might find some things you like over here.

Okay. Thanks.

Isabel turns to the rack nearest her. The dresses are from the 1930's, and some of them so delicate she can't imagine anyone but ghosts wearing them. Faded flowers, velvet trim worn down to the ribbon, buttons nodding at the floor.

She hears the shopkeeper tossing things around in her store-room. Something falls and the lady curses, but it's a stifled, antiquated curse Isabel can barely make out. Something like *bollocks*.

Found it! the lady calls. Oh, yes. This is the dress for you, my dear.

She emerges, triumphant, dress folded over her arm. When she reaches Isabel she holds the dress up by the shoulders. Creamy cotton with a print of teal and sapphire umbrellas with black handles. Sleeveless; full dancing skirt.

Isabel's heart leaps.

Sixties? she asks.

I think so, let's see. The lady peeks in the back by the zipper.

No label. If it had a label I could tell you where she bought it, and when—probably Meier & Frank—it's a classy, well-made dress. Early sixties, I would say, owing to that full skirt. But it's above the knee, and the pattern and cut around the shoulders say sixties for sure. Try it on.

She hands it to Isabel and gives her a nudge toward the dressing nook.

You bought it from an estate sale? Isabel asks, pulling the barkcloth curtain across the metal bar.

There is a string of Chinese lantern lights around the mirror and a little milkglass lamp with a fringed shade on a table. She lays the dress on an ottoman in the corner.

I bought the whole closet from the sister and brother-in-law of this woman, the shopkeeper tells her. A nice old house in North Portland.

She talks as Isabel undresses. Isabel hears the woman moving around, hanging clothes, her voice floating first near, then farther away, then back. The rattle of all the dresses on a rack shifting to make room for another.

Most of the clothes weren't very exciting, she continues. But there were a couple of dresses like this one and a really nice coat in some garment bags at the back of the closet. They obviously meant something to her—you don't keep a dress so long unless it means something to you. She probably met her first lover in that dress!

Isabel hears a muffled laugh as she pulls the dress over her head.

The cool fabric settles over her skin, and she thinks how this might be the first time in decades that a warm body has filled this space. She reaches behind her for the zipper and feels the fabric tighten around her as she draws it up to her mid-back, then the stretch perfectly across her shoulders as she tugs it the last few inches up her spine.

It's never the wedding dresses, you know. We keep those, too, but only because they're so blooming expensive. No. I've seen enough old ladies' closets to know what we *really* hold on to. Not the *till death do us* part dresses. It's those first lovely dresses: the slow dance dresses, the good night kiss dresses. It's those first pangs we hold on to.

Isabel turns to the mirror, bare feet pivoting on the geometric linoleum. In her reflection she can almost see the girl who wore the dress before her.

Architecture

Isabel had never smelled incense before she walked into her aunt's house. She was nine and Agnes was thirteen. Her mother's older sister taught astrology and couples communication at the Free School; her aunt's husband was a carpenter. Years later, a waft of nag champa will still send her back there: a big old house on a hill near Green Lake.

Isabel was weary, and followed Agnes across the threshold into the house watching the backs of her sister's aqua jelly sandals. The heady odor made her blink and raise her head. The was the living room with a saggy sofa, batik tapestries, books crammed into built-in shelves around the fireplace and in stacks on the floor by the TV. Worn oriental rugs overlapped on the beaten wood floors. The Astrologer led them to the guest room, where they heaped their bags on a mattress and box spring on the floor.

There were pictures of the Astrologer's guru— a smiling woman with short dark hair and a red bindi at her third eye—in almost every room. Isabel nudged Aggie to ask about them, but Aggie gave her a warning look, as if it would be rude to ask. There was a patchouli plant in the front window with tendrils stretched across the top of the television, through the rabbit ears. They left their doors open for the breeze and the bamboo blinds down over the windows, dicing the sunlight.

The Astrologer served them tea and coffee on a dining table she said had belonged to their great

great grandmother, Gigi, who was a flapper and married four times.

She and her sister had a little hair salon in their house in Mt. Vernon, the Astrologer said. During the week ladies would come get pin curls and have their finger waves set. Then on the weekends Gigi and Nell would drive all evening to get to the speakeasies in Seattle.

Isabel drank her chamomile from a delicate porcelain cup and after each sip carefully placed the cup back onto its saucer, trying not to spill. On the table sat a jar of honey with the comb suspended inside, sunlight suspended in the comb.

She had never seen a house like this before and she had never met people like the Astrologer and the Carpenter. The Astrologer wore long skirts and hand-dyed scarves around her hair, which was dark and curly, just like Isabel's mother's hair, but with more gray. She wore a rose quartz on a ribbon around her neck.

The Carpenter walked around barefoot, in threadbare T-shirts and running shorts. He asked Isabel lots of questions about herself—questions no one had ever asked her, like whether she liked living in Alaska and whether she would ever want to live anywhere else. She told him her grandmother had just gone to London and Dublin and sent her postcards. She wanted to travel to these cities someday. He nodded seriously when she answered, saying, *right on*, and holding eye contact long after both of them had finished speaking, until Isabel felt awkward and looked away.

They both treated Isabel and Agnes as if they were much older, as if it were okay to say *shit* in front of them, and to offer them sips of wine. They let Isabel play the piano in their dining room, though she didn't know how, and she felt obliged to make up songs on the spot; then they enthusiastically praised her musical talent.

At dinner they ate a vegetarian stew with eggplant and artichoke hearts. Their mother made a point to explain to Isabel and Agnes that these were vegetables that they couldn't get at home in Soldotna.

Mmm, said Agnes, pretending to like it.

Oh, said Isabel, trying to sound impressed.

Is that the bathroom faucet? the Astrologer said suddenly, setting down her glass of wine. They all listened intently, but no one seemed to hear anything. Then Isabel heard the faint trickle of water down a drain.

We have a ghost, the Carpenter said. He turns on the bathroom tap.

Isabel and Agnes stared at them.

Why? Agnes finally asked. Why would it do that?

He's just doing what he did when he was alive, the Astrologer said. Things he did over and over again, like walking the hallway to the bathroom and turning on the faucet.

Isabel went pale and dropped her fork.

Belly's afraid of ghosts, Agnes reported, as if *she* were not.

Well there's nothing to be afraid of, her aunt said, giving Isabel a sympathetic look. Ghosts are just energy, like an echo of someone's life.

Someone *dead*, Agnes said to Isabel.

Their mother elbowed Agnes to stop and forked a piece of eggplant from her younger daughter's plate.

Just think of it as an echo, their Aunt said. An echo can't hurt you, Isabel.

Isabel was skeptical. She avoided going to the bathroom all through dinner and dessert, until she couldn't contain all the tea in her bladder anymore.

She tread quietly into the dark living room, then the hallway, and to the bathroom door, ajar. She took a deep breath as she placed her hand on the crystal knob, reached inside for the light, and filled the room with a comfortable yellow glow. She shut the door and hurried to the toilet, then sat there, staring at the pink and black beehive tiles, begging her suppressed bladder to obey. Night had come, and the dark outside the frosted glass window loomed. She decided against washing her hands.

The next day, the Astrologer took them to Pike Place Market. They wandered through the sea of people, the shouts and reek of the fish mongers, the bright clutches of sweet peas in coffee cans. Then down the stairs into the belly of the market, a great hollow space like inside of a ship, with varnished wood plank floors that creaked and groaned with the waves of tourists.

There, in a long gallery of little shops, Isabel spied a sign that said, *Ephemera Maps & Photographs*.

What's that word? she asked, pointing to the sign.

What word? her aunt looked up. *Ephemera*?

Isabel nodded.

Ephemera means old paper things, old printed things. Do you want to see?

When they entered the shop Isabel thought of her photographs, and the shoebox at the Salvation Army Thrift Store. But this was a whole store full of old photographs, newspapers, magazines, postcards and even packets of letters. Isabel found a box of postcards and flipped through them, counting the cities she saw—Paris, Rome, Barcelona, Vienna— but couldn't decide which she wanted most.

She moved from box to box, picking up postcards and turning them over to read the captions. Agnes and her mother moved on to another shop, but the

Astrologer stayed, striking up a conversation with the man behind the counter. Isabel wanted to leave with something, but she wasn't sure what to choose. She had never seen such a selection of *ephemera* before.

In the back of the shop she found a box of postcards of Washington and Oregon: the Columbia Gorge, the Space Needle, trees and animals and coastline, the Canadian border. Then Isabel flipped to a scene she recognized: three Tlingit totem poles against a backdrop of spruce trees. She turned the card over: *Totem Bight near Ketchikan, Alaska*. She took the card to the counter, where a the Astrologer and the Shopkeeper looked at her expectantly.

Did you find something? her aunt asked.

Isabel nodded and lay the postcard on the counter in front of the shopkeeper.

How much is this postcard? she asked.

Let me see, he said, and picked it up carefully, turning it over and regarding it seriously from all sides.

This one is one dollar, he said.

Would you like it? her aunt asked.

Isabel pulled her beaded change purse from her pocket and counted out one dollar in quarters and dimes.

The man slipped the single postcard into a thin paper bag and handed it back to her.

Thank you, she said.

Enjoy, he said back quietly.

When Isabel's Agnes saw what she purchased she laughed at her sister and called her silly.

When you go on vacation you buy postcards of the place you're visiting, not the place you're from, Agnes told her.

Isabel was embarrassed, but stubborn enough not to show it.

I picked this one on purpose, she said. It reminds me of home.

Me, too, the Astrologer said, putting her arm around Isabel. I love things that remind me of where I came from.

That night after dinner, while the Carpenter worked out in the garage, the Astrologer brought Agnes, Isabel and their mother to her bedroom. They all sat on the bed while the Astrologer went into her closet for something. She emerged with a small wooden box. It had been decoupaged with colorful images of flowers from old greeting cards: voilets and pansies and forget-me-nots.

This was Grandma Gigi's, she said, resting it on the bed. She took a framed picture from her dresser and handed it to Agnes. Isabel leaned in to look. It was a matte print from the 1930s of a woman about their mother's age. The family resemblance wasn't obvious, but there the shape of the eyes and the nose looked like their mother and their aunt, and somewhat like Agnes.

The Astrologer went to her closet again and pulled out a dress—the dress Gigi wore in the photograph. It looked so small—too small for either of the grown women to wear—but small enough that Agnes might.

They spent the evening looking through old photographs and reading letters. Before they went to bed, their aunt opened up the little decoupaged box and revealed a few pieces of jewelry nestled carefully on a silk scarf.

She let the girls gaze into the box, then told them to pick one thing for themselves.

The girls looked at their mom, then at each other. There were glittery costume brooches, a mother of pearl bracelet, and a gold watch. But Agnes chose an amber pendant, that the Astrologer said had been a gift from Gigi's third husband, Vern. Isabel chose the smallest thing in the box, a garnet ring. It was too large for her, but she put it on her middle finger as she fell asleep that night, side-by-side on the mattress with her sister.

They talked in hushed voices about what it must have been like to live back then, and how lovely the clothes were and how exciting to have an adventuress in the family. They said that someday they would have daughters, and they would save precious things for them, too.

On the last day of their visit, they went for a walk in the Astrologer's neighborhood. They all enjoyed looking at the older houses, with their roses and wisteria and other flowers that you didn't see in yards in Alaska. The Carpenter pointed out different architectural features of the houses, and how differently houses would be designed today.

Most of the houses in this neighborhood are called Four-Square, he said, because of the rooms in each of the four corners of the house. They call them *Seattle Boxes* when the porch is under the second-story overhang like this—(he points to a house in the middle of the block). You could order a house from Sears, Roebuck and Company in those days—it came with everything you needed to build the house, from plans to shingles and floorboards to doorknobs. You could build it yourself or with your neighbors, or hire someone like me to do it for you.

They were back at their house, looking up the cracked cement stairs that curved up to their porch, the roses clambering over the picket fence, the lawn gone to seed and white clover.

You can always tell when something is handmade, the Astrologer said, sighing. They just don't make things like they used to.

Details

Next to the adult bookstore, a small door says: Vegetarian House, and underneath All Veg No Meat. A window on the street displays the menu, and a few Bible verses in Chinese and broken English. On the other side, one door down, is another restaurant with a steamy window and a case of rotating roast ducks.

Isabel steps inside the Vegetarian House and feels the moist quiet of the place. Clean, with whiff of moth balls. The first time she and Leo came here, a small cockroach walked down the wall nearly to their table, then scurried at the last minute onto a fake apple tree in the corner. The hollow papier-mâché apples and silk leaves glowed luridly beneath the insect. They watched it throughout their meal with good-humored detachment, calling her Oolong and addressing her in conversation. Whenever she recounts this story, people are astonished that she returns to eat here. But there is something about the place that she finds cozy and private. Off the crowded track of food carts, she can disappear briefly.

As she walks toward the tables, Isabel becomes aware that someone in the corner has looked up at her. She looks toward the apple tree and there is Spoke, staring at her, caught. He smiles, but Isabel feels caught as well. She smiles back and mouths *hello*, but realizes that they are alone in the restaurant. The waitress, the owner's wife (Isabel always assumed) recognizes her and gestures to Spoke.

Are you together? she asks.

Isabel looks from the woman to Spoke.

Yes? she says, to Spoke. He nods and she sits across from him at the small table. They shrug at each other almost simultaneously. They have never, in the last year, gone to lunch together—at least not alone, not to a restaurant. Everyone goes to the carts sometimes, of course, and will sit together in the park.

Spoke has already ordered, and his big bowl of rice and mock duck arrives. Isabel orders the tofu special and tucks the menu back in the napkin holder.

Though they often sit in the kitchenette, at the same table, with the salt shakers between them, where she can believe that the silence they share is mutually agreed upon, now, in a public place, mere inches apart, Isabel hopes one of them will start talking.

She could bring up the party, she thinks. Some words form themselves in her mouth. They regard

each other. She feels all of her abandoned places—
in her mouth, the tilt of her lower back, the bottom
of her lungs—but she cannot fill them. The space
around the two of them, sitting there together,
accumulates details in her mind. She imagines
the scene, as if they were in a play: the laminated
menus, hard vinyl chairs, plastic plants, spicy pickle
in glass jars with little metal spoons, partial light
through the window and fluorescent gleam from
overhead. Her looking at him, that same inscru-
table expression on his face, the way he looks her
in the eye, his parted lips, not quite saying what
he could say. All the buttons running down his
untucked red and blue plaid shirt. His sweater
hangs on the back of the chair.

It's so *warm* in here, she thinks. *Say something.*

Spoke isn't eating and she realizes this is probably
because she doesn't have any food yet, and he's being
polite. So she pours them both tea and they drink.

I didn't know you were a vegetarian, she finally gets out.

I'm not, Spoke says sheepishly, scratching his temple. I just feel like I ought to be sometimes.

Why do you think you ought to be? she asks.

Aren't you a vegetarian?

Since I was twelve, she says. But I guess I don't feel like everyone should be. Unless they feel compelled.

I guess sometimes I feel compelled, he says.

By what?

I spent a lot of time on farms, as a kid. I've seen a lot of animals up close.

Did you raise livestock?

No. I spent a lot of time—school vacations mostly—at my grandparents' farm, a few miles from Chippewa Falls, where I grew up. My grandpa was a veterinarian. He converted a barn on the family farm and had a practice there. For years he was the only vet for miles. People brought animals to him, and he drove around in an old pick-up visiting farms, treating livestock. When I was staying out at the farm, I rode along.

You watched him treat the animals? she asks.

Sometimes. Mostly I played with whatever kids were around, or sat in the back of the truck, waiting, reading comic books and Jules Verne. I guess it was just seeing what my grandfather did all day, caring for sick animals. He respected the animals—not like he ever talked about it, but I think he felt for them. I think he understood how powerless they were, how ultimately, everything is up to humans. We choose where they live, and how long, and, you know, what kind of sausage they become.

Isabel's food comes and they begin to eat.

Spoke looks out the window behind Isabel while he chews. They eat silently for a while, Spoke staring out the window, occasionally looking back to his bowl, then up at Isabel. Just when Isabel thinks the conversation is dead, he starts again.

It wasn't just animals, now that I think about it.

Isabel, mouth full of rice, cocks her head to the side and gives him a confused look. Spoke takes another bite and swallows.

We used to pick up junk off the side of the road—not actual trash, but dumped stuff. Washing machines and lamps and bicycles. We'd haul them back to my grandpa's shop and work on them till they were fixed—that's how I learned to fix things. If he didn't know how to fix it, he would send away for manuals and we would figure it out together. He just...wanted everything to last, or at least be given a chance.

Sounds like someone I could get along with, Isabel says.

She smiles at Spoke, but he just nods and looks seriously back at his lunch.

The waitress brings the little plastic tray with the bill and two fortune cookies.

Take your time, she says.

I wish I could, Spoke says mostly to Isabel.

Isabel looks up, surprised. He reaches for the bill.

I'll get yours, he says.

Thanks, she reaches for her wallet. But you don't need to do that.

I know I don't. But I want to, okay?

She gives him a questioning look, but he looks away.

Okay, she says softly.

He gets up and puts his sweater over his arm. His lips are red from the spicy pickle.

They have the best fortunes here, he says, picking a cookie from the tray.

Really? she says. She has never thought so.

They look at each other. She notices the buttons on his shirt again, pearly red buttons.

I'd better get back, he says, resolved. I have a meeting to get to.

She manages a small wave.

She sits by herself, unable to eat. She pours the last of the tea from the metal pot and sips. It is lukewarm, now, and she holds it in her mouth and lets it roll over her tongue. She cracks her fortune cookie and thinks of buttons. Small, pearly shirt buttons. The way they feel between your fingertips, against fingernails, slipping through cloth.

Fortunes

After lunch, heart lurching, she drops her bag and the cellophane sack from Lola's inside her office door, then walks down the hall to Spoke's office. She clutches her fortune in her hand.

His door is open and the room empty. She hesitates for a moment, then leaves the fortune on his desk so that he will find it when he gets back, a little scrap that says *You will attend a party where strange customs prevail*. Then she'll ask him to go with her to the party tonight. He was right, it was the best fortune she could have gotten.

In the hallway, she hears him on the stairs. She walks to her office door, and watches him, coming down with the head librarian, a tall woman in long, straight slacks who leans her head forward as she walks, as if she she's afraid she'll hit it on the ceiling.

—what we will do without you, she's saying. It just doesn't seem right to call you back, after you guys settle back into jobs and normal life. You've given so much already.

It takes Isabel a moment to realize what they're saying. Call you back. Called back.

Will you be in the battlefield, or somewhere safer? Working with computers, somewhere away from it all?

There are computers everywhere, he says to her.

Their boss seems agitated, her eyes red-rimmed. She likes Spoke; they all do.

He's going back, Isabel thinks. He's going back to the war.

She puts her hand on the doorframe. She gathers from the conversation that this has been in the works for a few weeks. He must have asked their boss not to tell them. He wanted to leave quietly. Come back to his job when this tour is done. Their boss is speaking so loudly she clearly thinks he has told everyone by now.

He looks up at Isabel as they pass, and adjusts his glasses. She is close enough to reach out and touch his arm, and she almost does, but pulls back. He looks at her and the color in his cheeks rises and she knows he is ashamed. The look she must be giving him. She doesn't care.

She wants to say, What did you think was going to happen? But she won't, not right now. She feels foolish. A sort of fury flows through her and makes her weak in the knees. Her heart pounding. Her little fortune on his desk, not sweet at all. Trying to flirt with him. He said nothing, this

109

morning, all week long. How long has he known? He would not look at her, stirred his coffee and did not look at her. Opened his mouth and did not tell her.

All the other office doors are open, all the seats turned toward the hall, no voices or typing, all the others listening. Ahmed, who shares Spoke's office, must have told some of them by now. He comes out of Nate's office, solemn. Nate follows. They both pause at the door, watching.

When Spoke and the head librarian have disappeared around the corner, Isabel watches Molly's freckled, manicured hand push open her door across the hall. Molly and Isabel look at each other.

Two women who mean nothing to the world, really, Isabel thinks. They stare at each other. The glow draining from Isabel's cheeks, the joy of the dress, folded into the little cellophane bag on her desk, gone. So trivial, that moment in the shop, in the mirror. He will never see her in the dress.

Molly's eyes widen and she mouths, *What the fuck?* As if Isabel should know. Molly's lipstick is worn away from lunch, her jaw clenched. She looks like she's about to blow up at someone.

Isabel could implode.

We mean nothing, she thinks, looking at Molly looking at her. We will survive and continue to mean nothing. He will go back to the war and kill or be killed. We might appear in his dreams along with girls who went to his high school, girls who lived next door, girls who shop and work and drink beer at summer parties, girls he slept with, or wanted to sleep with, girls who want to save him, or be saved by him. When he dreams of them he will open his mouth to speak and these girls will go off like bombs. Boom. Pieces of girls everywhere.

Isabel rests her head on her arm against the door. She stands there, staring down at her feet in her shoes on the cheap carpet for minutes—she loses track of time and breath—until Peter comes around to collect cash.

I'm going to the liquor store for whiskey. Let 'em write us up, he says, who gives a fuck?

Life in a Northern Town

Isabel wanted new things for a brief time, the spring after her tenth birthday. It was during her parents' divorce, but before she and Agnes knew that their mother was moving to New Mexico with a man named Steve, and that their father was applying for drafting jobs in Seattle and Portland.

It was a long division, Isabel would realize later. After his injury on the North Slope, their father started taking college classes on the weekends in Anchorage. He played in bar bands at night to make money. Their mother took a photography class at the community college on a lark, she said, to stay sane. When her parents were together, they had little to say to each other. The fissures in their family grew until the most important parts broke free and began to float away.

Agnes and Isabel felt the separation abruptly. One day, they were driving home from Pizza Paradiso in their dad's Chevy, the taste of root beer and oregano still on their lips, and the next they were dividing everything between their little house by woods and the apartment in town their mother had rented.

Isabel still remembers packing day. She and Agnes wandered around their room, choosing this toy and that book and a favorite dress or blouse. They dropped them into cardboard boxes onto which their mother had written, in purple magic marker, each of their names. Isabel found herself staring into her box at her belongings, noticing how different they looked, like they had lost all meaning to her.

Agnes talked about going to the mall in town to meet her friends, and for once Isabel wanted to tag along. Agnes occasionally skulked into the kitchen to whine at their mother, who insisted they stay home and pack. Isabel and Agnes had never fought much, but they were so different, in looks and in personality, that they rarely found reasons to bond. Isabel suddenly felt the urge to join in her sister's crusade.

Please, Mom, they said. We're nearly done. How much longer do we have to do this? This is our weekend. Don't we get to do anything fun?

When they went back their bedroom Agnes gave Isabel approving looks and helped her pack clothes so that they could finish quickly.

Back in the kitchen they started again.

Finally Agnes unleashed: Why does your divorce have to ruin everything for us?

Yeah, Isabel said, following her sister's lead.

Their mother threw the Tupperware she was holding into the box at her feet. She stared at her daughters for two long breaths. Her curly hair was springing out of the bandana she had tied over it that morning in a perfect kerchief. Her eyes were red and her lips chapped.

Fine! she yelled, her voice quivering. Just get in the damn car.

At the mall, their mother planted herself on a bench by the entrance with a diet soda and *The Shell Seekers* while the Isabel silently tailed Agnes. The mall didn't have much to offer: a drugstore, a candy shop and a Baskin-Robbins, the Book Cache, which sold bestsellers and greeting cards, a shoe store, a sporting goods shop, a Sears catalog kiosk with a row of rotary phones to place orders directly with operators, and a J. Jacobs, which catered to teenagers.

Agnes met her friends there. They were all thin and pretty, with their ears pierced and their hair curled and sprayed up in waves over their foreheads. They gave Isabel a cursory glance as she lingered beside Agnes. Agnes gave her an apologetic look and Isabel took the hint. She set off wandering the store, looking here and there at the trendy clothes, watching Top 40 videos on the big TV above the register.

Agnes and her friends made straight for the formal wear, gushing over the metalic pink bubble skirts and heart-shaped tops. The spring formal at Soldotna Junior High was just weeks away. Isabel caught a glimpse of Agnes holding a silky peach dress up to her body, peering down at herself while her friends cooed. Isabel knew their mother would never let Agnes wear the dress—J. Jacobs was *cheap*, she had said before, and not in a price way—she rarely let Agnes buy so much as a T-shirt.

Isabel watched the videos: Debbie Gibson and the New Kids on the Block. She turned at a rack of jeans and came face to face with herself in the mirrored far wall: tattered ponytail, shabby pink windbreaker, her sister's old jeans rolled up at the ankles and dirty sneakers. She could hear the urgent, secretive talk and gurgling laughter of the older girls in the dressing rooms and she suddenly understood why her sister like to come here and try on beautiful dresses she could never buy. It was like trying on another life.

Isabel walked back through the store, keeping an eye out for something—anything—she thought she might wear. She settled on a hot-pink, short-sleeved knit top with buttons along the right shoulder. She took a size small from the rack and walked past her sister without making eye-contact, straight into a dressing room.

What are you doing, Belly? Agnes called.

Isabel pulled the curtain shut without responding. She took off her wind-breaker and the white Anchorage Zoo T-shirt she wore underneath. She slipped the new shirt from its hanger and pulled it over her head.

Isabel, you know mom won't buy that, Agnes said quietly from the other side of the curtain.

The new shirt felt so soft draped on Isabel's shoulders. The knit fabric was loose and fell below her hips, almost like a dress. There was a flowery aroma to it that was nothing like the Mule Team Borax smell of her hand-me-downs and thrift store shirts.

Belly? Agnes poked her head through the curtain. She looked at Isabel and smiled.

Too bad, she said. It's pretty cool.

Back Pocket

She waits, fusses with papers in her office, slowly gathers her bag and sweater, composing them on her arm carefully, so that she can walk out with him. One by one the others leave. She listens to all their goodbyes.

The afternoon passed in a stunned, vacant stare. At first they all pretended to work—Spoke busy becoming absent, removing everything he brought with him—then their boss went upstairs and they didn't bother. Isabel stayed on the edge, just out of reach.

At four o'clock they all gathered in the break room and poured whiskey into mugs for a mostly awkward farewell toast.

Ahmed, always one to speak for others, gave a short, graceless speech about the fucked-up beauty of America, which concluded:

It's pretty much a mixed bag, you know? But you're one of the good ones. We need you in the mix.

Isabel stood across from Spoke, silent. Spoke smiled amiably, listened, but seemed to Isabel like a door slowly swinging closed over a worn arc of floor. When he looked at Isabel—their eyes meeting across the table for the last time—she tried to smile but tears filled her eyes, and he looked away.

Isabel's office is the last on the way out of the building, so she watches each of her friends leave. Nate nods at her as he passes. Peter says, What a fucking day, and Isabel agrees with her eyes. Molly picks up her things from her office, then drops them in the middle of the hallway and grabs

Isabel, hugging her. Isabel lifts her arms and wraps them around her until Molly suddenly pulls away, wipes her nose on her sleeve, picks up her belongings and heads quickly up the stairs and out the door. Ahmed is the last to go, shaking his head. They all leave him where they will remember him, and Isabel thinks that she could have done that, too. She could leave without a word, after his silence all day, all month.

She listens to him leaving. Waits in her office door, staring at the floor, until she hears his footsteps turn in her direction. He stops next to her, leaning on the wall.

You were waiting for me, he says.

I was? She tries to be coy but it comes out with too much emotion behind it and sounds angry and defensive.

Sorry, she says. I'm not very good with subtlety.

No, he says. But your way is better.

He reaches into the back pocket of his jeans and pulls out her fortune. She feels herself blush, seeing the way he holds it in his palm, examines it.

I didn't know, she says. I'm going to a party tonight—I thought you might come with me. It seems—I don't know—shitty now.

How could you have known?

He reaches into his pocket again and pulls out an identical, tiny slip of white paper with red print. He hands it to her.

Your journey will take you to faraway places.

Her mind gets stuck on the word *faraway*. Faraway is one word? she thinks.

She holds the fortune in her hand, unsure whether he means to give it to her.

He puts her fortune back in his pocket. So she does the same with his. Then he gestures to the door and they start walking toward the stairs. They pause at the top, his hand on the metal door latch.

He seems to be considering what he should say to her. She thinks about what is on the other side of the door: a postcard of a city.

She curls her hair behind her ear. He shifts his bag to the shoulder opposite her.

Walk with me? he asks.

Okay, she nods.

Around the building and down the brick steps. He unlocks his bike and they walk away together through their city, the ticking of his bike keeping time.

Can I ask you a question? she says.

Yeah.

Pausing at a corner as the commuter train pulls to a stop in front of them. When he looks at her she feels a crash inside, pieces of her breaking off and floating away.

How did you end up in the army? she asks.

She doesn't know why but out it comes. It is a confession: of all those things she thought about soldiers before she met him; that she loves with him and cannot fathom why he would want to kill people and risk his life like this.

He looks up the sidewalk, measuring some distance up the street.

Do you even know? she asks. Stepping off the curb, he lifts his bike and she watches their feet descend, her black leather slip-on next to his worn sneaker.

He stops, looks at her, everything they've never said flowing into this narrow space between them. Isabel feels the passing of time acutely, like a flood coming and only so much time to gather up the most important things.

He stops short in the middle of the sidewalk, under the awning of a magazine and tobacco shop. She looks up at him, thinking how tall he is, how her nose would fit neatly into his clavicle if she walked right into him. A few people walk around them, pass. If she were other people, she would be silently telling them to *fucking move, yous*, but she doesn't care. The streetlights have changed, leaving them alone on this stretch of city block. Pigeons scuttle around a trash can, then begin to wander nearer their unmoving feet.

I didn't feel like I had many options, he says finally. I wanted experience and I wanted to get out of my hometown for a while.

That's an answer. Is it true?

Yeah. Yes. All true.

But that doesn't tell *me*, she says.

It's a long story, he says.

I want the long story.

He just looks at her, and for a minute she thinks he might kiss her. Then he nods and they walk.

The food vendors across the street are packing

up their carts, washing down their counters and tables, cooling off in the breeze, sipping sodas or having a smoke.

Their arms touch and her skin vibrates. He pulls away slightly. Maybe he doesn't want to be so close to her, she thinks. Or maybe he does not want her to know how much he wants to touch her.

So she moves closer to him, again, letting her bare arm brush against his. He doesn't move away this time.

Thaw

When Isabel was very small her father worked on the North Slope for what seemed like months at a time. It was actually two weeks on, two weeks off, but time seemed to go on longer then.

In the winter, the Slope was a dark, starry place, with a colony of busy fathers working in the snow and ice. In the summer, the light never ended and they measured one hour to the next by the beeps on their digital watches, eating periodically from vending machines. Isabel knew about the vending machines because when her father came home he always brought a candy bar for Agnes and Isabel to share.

The girls couldn't sleep summer nights, because of the light slipping in from outside. And on nights when their father was coming home, they waited up for him and the candy bar. She remembers running into his arms; the cold petroleum smell of his work clothes.

But when they asked questions about where he had been and what he had been doing, he said very little. Only their mother told them what they wanted to know about oil underground and the dividend checks the family received every year.

One winter night, their father came home early. His left hand was wrapped in bandages like a fat white mitten. There had been an accident; his hand was smashed. After a couple of days, they removed the bandages to take pictures, pictures Isabel can still draw up in her mind: horizontal blue lines where fingernails should be; swollen, flat, crooked fingers that all curved the same direction at the middle joint.

Daddy, why are your fingers going west? Isabel asked. Having just learned how to use a compass, she believed left was always west.

There was no answer. He thought he would never play guitar again.

Years later, in Portland, their father began to tell them his stories. They trickled out of him, as if his past were slowly melting: the early days of long winters snowed in at the homestead; his father shooting the first moose to wander down the driveway in the fall; moose sandwiches for months; working summers as a teenager, cleaning trash and outhouses in camp grounds (banging an big aluminum spoon against the garbage pails to frighten off bears); leaving home at sixteen to play music with feckless friends; his father getting their band a gig at a bar (brothel) in Kenai, not asking how his father knew the owner (Madam); searching piles

131

of fish heads for a human hand his last summer at the cannery; the fishing boat he sank all his money into; the friend who sank the boat; and eventually, working on the North Slope.

There were only two places to work, he said: the canneries or the Slope. He had worked both. It was an explanation and an apology. Though for what, Isabel still wasn't sure. He always seemed to be flying away from them when they were little girls. Isabel thought that he believed this was the reason their mother stopped loving him. That was an easy explanation, but the apology was more complicated.

There was the pipeline and the oil that thrummed through it. There was evidence of harm all around—as close as the end of his arm. Beyond: there was the spill that coated the sea and the coastline and all the animals there. Then there was the thaw, the threateningly deep, vast thaw: a lucid dream of a legacy for children who know better but cannot stop it.

Isabel cannot read magazine articles or books about the North. She cannot watch the nature programs about the migrations of birds and mammals dwindling, the sea ice thinning, and the erosion of islands. And she does not want to know what has happened to her great-grandmother's house by the woods, sold years ago to people who let gutted cars rot in the front yard.

When she thinks about her northern childhood now, she thinks of her father, flying to the Slope with all the other fathers, toiling over the permafrost. She sees him in his work coat and heavy boots, hardhat over a woolen skullcap, slipping coins into the slot of a vending machine, pressing the button and hearing the clink and the drop, reaching his undamaged left hand through the metal flap for the candy bar.

Rest and Gladness

She stares at the windowsill in his apartment: spores and insect husks. She hears him at the sink, then his footsteps across the room. He stops next to her and looks out the window and hands her his cold, scuffed metal water canister.

She smiles thanks.

Sorry I can't offer you anything else, he gestures to the nearly empty room.

Where did you sleep last night? she asks.

Sleeping bag.

They sit on a camp blanket spread under the window, and look into the room together.

She drinks and hands the bottle to Spoke, who takes a long swig. Isabel watches the way his throat expands and contracts as he swallows. She is closer to him than she has ever been. She notices more about his face. He lets his beard grow a little, so that from a distance the skin beneath disappears. Now she is so close she can see the individual whiskers, which are brown and red and blonde, and the skin underneath.

My parents are college professors, he says.

Isabel lifts an eyebrow. He has never mentioned them.

They really wanted me to go to college right away after high school. But I kind of hated school. I liked to read, I was a curious kid. I just hated school. I wanted to be outside doing something.

The last summer I spent at my grandparent's place was a compromise. They let me take a year to decide where I wanted to go to college. I was

supposed to help my grandpa with the property— there was a small orchard that hadn't been tended much since my grandma died, fix things around the house, drive him to the store and church.

But he died that fall. One morning, he wasn't up before me. I found him in bed and couldn't wake him. He'd had a stroke in the night. He died later, in the hospital.

You were really close, she says.

Yeah.

Is that why you wanted to leave?

No. I wanted the farm. I wanted to live there and run the orchard. But my parents didn't think I had the resources or experience. They told me I could go to ag school if I wanted to be a farmer. My dad sold the house, the orchard, all the equipment. Everything.

Isabel watches Spoke, the way he runs the tips of his fingers over the seam on the side of his jeans.

She can almost feel the ridge in the fabric herself.

I signed my enlistment papers the day they closed probate, he says.

Why? she asks.

I knew they were right—I was pissed—but I knew they were right. It was more about my grandpa and what he went through in the war, and what it was like for him after my Grandma died.

This is the long story, he says.

He never talked about the war, Spoke says. But when it came up, he would get somber and say something like, *There are some things in the world so broken they can't be fixed.*

Spoke gazes off into the room as he speaks, looking to Isabel at the ends of sentences, as if to make sure she is still there. Isabel's eyes drift around the room, but listens to his voice and tries to picture the place he grew up.

He tells her about his grandfather, silent and

stoic in a typically midwestern way, but gentle, and devoted to his wife. They were the only people he'd ever known who were truly in love. He remembers sitting at the kitchen table, eating a big slice of cake, his grandmother singing *O Day of Rest and Gladness* as she washed dishes. His grandfather would come in for lunch, wrap his arms around her waist, and kiss her, once, right at the curve of her neck.

She looks to Spoke and sees that he's blushing slightly. He looks back at her nervously. It's such an intimate detail, she knows he has never told anyone. She can't help but imagine him kissing her in the same place, and she feels heat tingle through her chest and neck and rise to her cheeks.

There was something secret between his grandparents, he continues. Something that connected the two of them in a way no one else could ever understand.

He pauses again. The room is silent, except for the drip of the kitchen faucet into the old porcelain sink.

Then he goes on: She died when he was twelve.

He remembers waking one morning in his dad's childhood bedroom—months after his grandmother's funeral—the house was silent, cold. He pulled on an overcoat and boots and wandered out into the yard. It was spring—the final thaw over, everything muddy and green and steaming in the morning sun. When he got to his grandfather's shop he stopped. He could see his grandpa through a crack in the door, sitting on his work stool, crying, quaking. He had never seen him cry—not in all the weeks that had passed, not even at the funeral. There was a box of letters open on the workbench. He assumed they were from his grandmother, from during the war, before they were married.

He snuck back to the house and just stood in the kitchen, staring at the sink. Everything was different, with her gone. It wasn't even like half of his grandparents were gone, it was like his grandmother took part of him with her. Spoke didn't know what to do. That there wasn't a pot of coffee on—she always made it, even though she didn't drink it—so Spoke pulled the big can down from the cupboard and made a pot in the percolator. He didn't know how, so he filled the basket with grounds—it came out thick and muddy. But when his grandfather finally came in from the shop he poured a cup and drank it all, sitting at the table with Spoke, not saying anything.

Before his father sold the farm, Spoke spent one last night in the house. When he woke in the morning he made coffee for himself in the percolator and sat at the kitchen table, drinking it alone. Then he pulled on his grandpa's old denim and sheepskin coat and went out to the shop. He searched for close to an hour before he found the box of letters—the his grandfather read after his wife died. It was an old wooden cigar box, with a tiny rusted lock that Spoke had to jimmy with a small screw driver.

Spoke looks back at Isabel, brow furrowed.

They weren't letters from my grandmother to my grandfather, he says. They were letters from him to her. His regiment was at the surrender of Dachau. He described the whole grisly scene— what we grew up seeing in movies and history books, but worse, because it's in this naïve farm-boy's words—comparing the prisoners to veal calves, things like that.

Isabel grimaces.

But they were love letters, too. Spoke's grandfather wrote about her—his random thoughts of her, remembering the dress she wore the last evening they spent together, how she was like a dream to him because he thought of her every night, sometimes intensely, shutting out everything around him just to imagine her face and hands and voice, but when he woke she was not there with him. All of this was there in that kiss, witnessed by the little boy in the kitchen. He survived the war, and woke up every morning afterward to his dream.

Spoke falls silent, leans back into the wall and rubs his hands over his face.

Isabel looks at her hands in her lap.

Don't go, she says. You already survived once.

She realizes that she is about to cry. She stands up suddenly, her knees aching and weak from sitting on the floor for so long, and stumbles. Spoke jumps up and puts out a hand to steady her.

She grasps him, rests her forehead on his chest. Spoke, who drinks his coffee from a mason jar and fixes things and thinks he ought to be a vegetarian. She closes her eyes and kisses him. It startles her, how warm he is, how much breath the kiss takes. He places his hand on the back of her head and cradles her head in his palm. She reaches for the hem of his shirt, slips beneath it and slides her hand over his belly. She navigates the crenellation of his rib cage slowly until she feels the burst of flesh that must be his scar, soft tender folds around a stippled center, like a pressed flower. He kisses her neck and his beard leaves thousands of tiny abrasions on her skin.

Exit, Glacier

Isabel walked right up to the glacier. She could hear it sighing and dripping. She put her warm plump hand on the heaving lung of it. She could feel its breath and the minute spaces inside filling with water and the great creases pulling in the sky.

It was their last camping trip before they moved away. Isabel and Agnes had each invited a friend, and they played the usual games: Hearts and War, for cards; and a divining game with paper and pencil, called MASH, which stood for Mansion Apartment Shack House. MASH revealed a girl's future husband, car, city of residence and abode. Isabel would be married to Matt Jones (a catch, by fifth grade standards), who would drive an El Camino, to their House in Nashville. They played these games into the waning hours of the day, when the low, long sun cast their shadows into each other.

When they tired of games, they told the same scary stories over and over.

Isabel played the games and shared the stories, but she felt too old to enjoy them. She felt outside of herself, removed from her childhood, as if watching it all from behind a tree several feet away. Sometimes her sister looked at her from across the campfire, and Isabel understood that Aggie felt the same way.

They toasted s'mores, and looked out into the dark woods, and up at the every star in the northern sky. Their mother and her friend, Pam, drinking warm beer by the fire. The girls finally fell asleep, berry-stained, mosquito-pocked, hands cold.

On the last day, Isabel begged to make the hike to the glacier again—it wasn't far. They drove to where the dirt road folded into itself at a rusted red gate, then walked the rest of the way over the path through the woods. Then the trees suddenly drew back and there it was: Exit Glacier, like a ghost in the mirror. As uncanny and startling as anything, even for an Alaskan girl. Isabel clambered over centuries of rocks, all heaved from the glacier's embrace. She stood beneath it, wobbly-knees and pink windbreaker, for a photograph. Then she turned, spread her goose-pimpled arms wide and pressed her warm lips to it.

Adrift

In her bedroom she tosses her shoes to the closet floor and opens the window to let in a breeze and a wash of light. The cat perches herself on the sill, washing her face with a paw.

Isabel pulls her dress out of the little cellophane bag from the vintage store. She lays the dress out across the end of her bed, skirt just falling down the side, then digs a pair of black open-toed heels from the closet and places them on the floor below, so that it looks like an invisible girl is stretched out there. She thinks of the postcard girl, taking her place at the party. What did she do the night her lover flew away?

She's sleepy, after the long walk home. Heat in her head and limbs. She undresses down to her bra and underwear and climbs onto the bed next to the clothes to rest for just a moment, before she gets ready for the party. She sinks onto the cool quilt.

It was almost a wordless goodbye. They stood on his stoop. He hugged her to him and the tears in her lashes left wet marks on his plaid shirt. The pearly red buttons pressed to her cheek.

She took his face in her hands and gave him a long hard stare.

He just nodded.

She let her hands fall and stepped back.

Bell, he says.

Hm?

You owe me a story.

When?

Whenever.

In her half sleep she confuses the wanting of him and the missing of him. The same way she thinks of Amsterdam almost as if she has been there, and longs to return. Too much of Spoke belongs to a place that does not actually exist, a city just like this one, except that in the other city they have been lovers for weeks, had their first fight and eaten food from each other's plates. It might as well be Amsterdam.

Her eyes close and she begins to drift. She thinks how of these things: Spoke and the war, how he will kill people and might be killed himself; the oil in Alaska and the oil in the Middle East; the glaciers melting, and the water that connects it all. The glaciers will melt and the water will rise. Everything will be washed through. All the young lovers in their hats and their summer dresses. All the plane-trees and the elms. All the tall houses. All the narrow brick lanes and city squares. Glaciers take the cities, cities take the architecture, the architecture takes the bodies.

When she wakes, she focuses on the chair and the cellophane bag, then clothes thrown over the foot of the bed, as inanimate as ever. Her eyes are salt-dried and she is thirsty.

She rises and lurches to the bathroom where the sea glass light through the frosted window tells her she has slept too long.

She draws a bath.

The cat perches on the back of the toilet.

A slip she washed in the sink a week ago still hangs from a towel bar, where it dried, bent at the waist.

She pulls her underwear off, lifting one bare foot then the other from the cold tile floor. She tilts, a hand lifting to steady herself, reaching for an anchor.

All Dressed Up

The bus pulls away from the curb and starts over the bridge. The sun has set behind the city, all shadows against what's left of the light. The last wash of dusk behind the west hills and all the smaller lights (the rooftop gardens and office windows and neon signs) shimmering drunkenly in the river.

She has questions, for example: Can soldiers check their e-mail? Do they still receive packages from old ladies with notes of encouragement and hand-knit scarves? If I sent him a pair of my panties could he trade them for booze and M & M's?

The bus descends into downtown between the great neon Made In Oregon sign and the red and white shield of the Salvation Army.

She pulls the cord for her stop by the strip club that used to be a Cuban restaurant. She steps off the bus and avoids the pile of trash overflowing the garbage can there. The wind nudges her along and the skirt of her new dress, the one that made the shopkeeper sigh, dances around her legs. She shoves her hands into the pockets of her sweater.

Blocks away his apartment settles, while he waits in a terminal for a plane.

At the door she reaches for the bell, but draws her hand back. She looks up at the tall narrow brick building. Lights spill out. It looks warm and sparkly. The sounds of voices and laughing trickle from the windows above. A few words: *gondoliers, capitalism,* and *treehorn.*

Leo would be wondering. He relies on her to save him from regrettable trysts and morbid hangovers. She, on the other hand, could do something impulsive and hedonistic. Something he would whole-heartedly endorse. She could go back home, pack a suitcase and call a taxi for the airport. She could put a plane ticket on her credit card. She would text him: gone to AMS please feed cat don't fret will call soon.

But no.

She raises her hand and pulls the bell. Footsteps down the stairs behind the ornate wooden door, closer and closer. She could still slip around the corner and out of sight. She knows these people, even if she has never met them. These people will make her dance, get her good and drunk without remorse, and know nothing about the man who should be there with her. (She looks up at the sky, as if to catch a glimpse of an airplane passing.)

Then the door opens and here is Leo, happy to see her.

I knew it was you, he says.

He raises an eyebrow as if to say, *Well, where is he?* He looks around pointedly. But he knows better than to ask out loud.

I'm late, she says lamely.

You're *here*, he says.

He holds the door and gives her a kiss as she crosses the threshold.

New dress? he asks.

New dress, she says.

Other People's Stories

Isabel always forgets how much she loves Theater People. And the party is rotten with them, as her mother would say. They fill her with drinks and have conversations spoken in accents, faux and real. They are the only people she knows who have ever been impressed that she met Harvey Fierstein's mother once. But the best part is the stories. They love to tell stories and to pull them out of others. Or maybe this only happens at Michael's parties.

Michael calls his loft the Castle, though it was a casket factory until the 1970s. He's giving a tour as Isabel and Leo enter the room, to a wide-eyed young woman with bright red lipstick and a chic black dress.

The ingénue, Isabel thinks.

And this is where they stacked the finished coffins, Michael says, gesturing to the kitchen.

Michael has an overdeveloped sense of historical significance, Leo whispers to Isabel.

That must be why I like him, Isabel replies.

During the war, Michael continues as they pass, there was such a need for coffins that they filled the whole room and actually started passing them through the windows and lowering them down to the street with pulleys.

Which war? Isabel turns to Leo for an answer.

He shrugs.

There are no doors in the main room, only a broad stairway from below, and windows, hemming the room at either end like great headstones, wedged and solid and curved at the top, fragments of signs and billboards outside. They are all tall enough to be doors, the sills wide enough to stand on, and wide enough for caskets to pass through, Isabel thinks.

Isabel and Leo make drinks, then seat themselves on a window sill to watch the party.

After a moment he asks: So, what happened?

She looks at Leo. Really looks at him, for the first time in weeks. He has lost weight again, she thinks. Smoking too much and eating not enough. She can still see the adolescent in him, and sometimes she envies his ability to forge into the future, while she feels compelled to carry the with the past.

He had to go back, she says finally.

Go back?

To the woods.

There are period sofas and chairs—many eras, all set pieces, she's sure—scattered around the loft.

Isabel finds herself a vacant one and settles herself while Leo has a cigarette on the fire escape.

Michael appears. He holds out his hand.

Oh no, she says. My feet are a little sore. Actually, they're wrecked. I've walked the city and back today.

Isabel, it would be a disgrace to that dress, he says, grabbing her hand.

The music is loud and percussion heavy. She cannot demur. She lets tall Michael lead her around the room, practically carrying her, lifting her off her feet in an improvised waltz. She loses a shoe. Faces turn toward them as Michael ferries her through conversations, interrupts drunken courting. They are sanguine, dreamy, cocktail-soaked faces. More dancers join, anachronistic dance moves erupt. She loses her other shoe. She laughs until her eyes are wet and Michael releases her to the wood planks, barefoot, telling her to watch for splinters, and then turns to a startled young man in a baby blue button-down shirt and sweeps him off his feet. He has dropped Isabel at the green velvet sofa where Leo has settled with a red-headed young man. *His* red-headed young man, she thinks. She runs her hands along her dress and falls next to Leo with a poof of her skirt.

Catch your breath, he says.

Hours sift through her. She feels whiskey-warm and almost grateful. Occasionally she leans out a window for air, counting stars, watching for the blinking lights of airplanes. Anyone out in the street, looking up at the old casket factory, would see her perched at the window, a merry ruckus behind her.

Then, at some point, a hush. Quietly, one voice then another, over the ledge, out the open windows, into the night street, where the last bus passes on its way across the river, where two gutter punks walk with their dog, and a couple slip away from the late-night crepe shop and speakeasy.

She turns back into the room. The others are piled onto the chairs and sofas. Half-empty glasses, dirty plates and forks. Crusts of bread smeared with savory pastes. A space cleared where two rise to demonstrate a jig. Two men who watched each other from across the room all night, leaning together now, one against the other, like fallen columns in ancient ruins. A playwright, and a musician, and a filmmaker, and a few actors, and a waiter who once modeled for Hedi Slimane, and some lovers and former lovers, all resting around a low table with a lopsided red velvet cake, white frosting glowing, wound gaping, recumbent smeared forks. They gather around a few candles and drink what's left of the bottles. They are all friends now, those who have made it this late into the night.

Isabel, Michael calls. Come seat yourself, it's story time.

Isabel crosses the room and curls up on the floor against a sofa.

Let's all tell a story we've never told anyone before.

What kind of story? the Model asks.

I'm not much of a storyteller, the Ingenue claims.

How about this, Michael says, leaning back into his velvet armchair. I'm the host, so I will tell you what kind of story to tell. It doesn't have to be long, it doesn't even have to be good. Just let it be *true*.

He turns to the Model.

Adam, he stares into the young man's face. Tell us a Bittersweet story.

Adam stares seriously at the floor for a long, silent time. Then he looks up and says: Rhubarb.

When he was a boy, he had the peculiar luck of finding dead animals everywhere: crows, robins, squirrels, shrews and, once, four newborn kittens in an overturned box in the woods.

He would run home for a rag or some newspaper, then return to the animals, carefully gather them up, and take them home.

His mother told him to bury them, but not *where* to bury them, so he chose the spot in the garden by the rhubarb. Rhubarb was the first harvest from the garden every spring. They made pies and jam and syrups. The jeweled jars lined the bottom shelf of the lazy susan all year. Rhubarb was also the one edible thing in the garden his mother didn't forbid him from picking. He would yank the stalks up, strip off the poisonous leaves, pour some sugar into his palm and dip the stalks in it, sucking the bitter-tart-sweet juice.

When he laid the animals down in the soil, he said the same prayer for each of them: *I hope you find your way, friend.* Then he covered them with soil and a small bouquet of whatever flowers he could find.

He would think of them every time his mother sent him to fetch a jar from the Lazy Susan.

The Ingenue is next.

Paige, tell a story about . . . Regret.

So she tells a story about visiting England in college. She had a chance to visit the river in which a beloved writer drowned. She had a mousy friend with a family cottage nearby. But she wanted to desperately to be fashionable. So instead she went to London to see a boy who later humiliated her— the only time in her life she'd ever been called a cunt—at a party full of people she thought she wanted to impress.

She pauses here, and then the story turns.

Her mother used to tell her she looked like someone else's child. She used to sit in her mother's lap and ask her questions. Did she have her eyes? Her nose? Her mouth? Her hands? Her voice? And the answer was always, no, no. Her mother said, You must be a changeling. But all she wanted to be was her mother's daughter. She remembers her mother's face from the angle of her lap. The smell of her shampoo, and the hairs on her arms. She tells it like this, the river, London, the boy, and her mother.

Then the overseas call to her mother, asking for airfare home. And her mother saying, no. No.

Then comes Jacob, the painter, whose story must be about Decay.

Jacob's mother worked at the old insane asylum. Years later, when the building was no longer in use, the painter befriended the nightshift security guard at the local tavern. He was a young man just like the painter, who took on the job because he needed work, though it terrified him. The painter asked again and again to visit during the guard's rounds, but the guard always refused—he could get fired, and besides—he'd trail off, shaking his head and staring into his beer. After a few, the guard would start talking about the place. The sounds and smells of it. The graffiti and detritus. The way he couldn't eat his lunch with his back to the station door. And the painter felt a thrill at the idea of visiting the place, an almost erotic desire to witness the remains of the building and what its occupants left behind.

Then, one day, the guard decided he couldn't do it anymore. He told the painter to come for his last night on the job and he would show the painter what horrible place it was.

The painter parked at the gate and stood at the chain link fence, waiting. He waited twenty minutes. He watched the building for movement, for a sign of his friend. He watched the surrounding fields. He watched the cars on the freeway in the distance, and the lights of the houses in the suburb a few miles away blink on and off.

There was a ditch on the side of the road, the kind from his childhood, when they lived on the bad side of the tracks in a small town. He remembered one spring when the thaw happened so quickly that the ditches filled up with water, and the neighborhood children, exhilarated by the sudden heat, had stripped to their underwear and jumped in the muddy ditch. He remembered the feel of the warm mud between his toes and the murky water, and the way his mother just shrugged when she saw him there, in the ditch with the other children. She often slept on the sofa in the middle of the day, waking up periodically to smoke cigarettes and watch the soaps before she left for the asylum.

Waiting at the gate for his friend, he thought of his mother, the same age then as he was now, pulling up to this gate in her red Chrysler. Her hair was strawberry blonde, and she wore a medal of St. Christopher on a silver chain. He thought about her walking through the front doors, through the halls, cleaning up body fluids, tying sick people to their beds, witness to their shock treatments and nightmares.

The guard finally came, and they walked through the gate, up the steps. As the guard opened the door, shining his flashlight around the dead corridor, the painter realized he couldn't do it. He couldn't walk through the doors. After all that.

Then it's Leo's turn.

Leo, Michael says. Leo, also known as Loon by people who love him. Loon, tell us a Haunting story.

So Leo tells them about a recent dream. In the dream he was obsessed with the movie *Night of the Hunter*. But it wasn't *Night of the Hunter*. It was an old vampire movie with Theda Bara in it. In fact, it was called *Return of the Hunter*, a sequel to *Night of the Hunter*. He was watching it on his grandmother's old television. The one with the knob to turn from channel to channel and the rabbit ears. It was cased in wood, and was so large and heavy that it sat on the floor, the largest piece of furniture in the room. But this was not in his grandmother's living room. It was in an older house, a castle he was visiting in Wales. It was a moonless night. The furniture was growing its own upholstery. Armchairs and couches were alive, like plants. Mossy. Fungal. He didn't want to sit on anything. There was a kitchen nearby with people preparing food from boxes and cans. Leo watched the vampire movie, thinking to himself that he must remember to find this movie later, in daylight, back in his city.

In the movie a woman stood in a dark room, blood smeared her collar bones. Tears streaked the kohl around her eyes. The film was black and white, but the blood was red, and Leo thought, *brilliant*, because his dream self thought this an amazing feat for early twentieth-century filmmaking. He felt afraid, like a child, as if he shouldn't be watching this, as if he should run into the kitchen, to be safe in the company of others. But he realized this was important, this film. That all the other movies he had seen, or would ever see, would not affect him so much as this one. She was alone and she was going to die an ugly, painful death. Then she was dead and he watched small children dressed in black suits and dresses open and close their mouths over pointed, sharp teeth.

He walked into another dream, a dream in which *Return of the Hunter* still existed, and he occasionally thought he should find it and watch it again.

So the stories come and go, one after another. Leo and Isabel watch each other across the circle.

Isabel's legs bent to her side, head in her hand, elbow propped on the corner of the sofa. Her slip is showing, her hair falling out of bobby pins. He looks like a kid, she thinks, hugging his knees to his chest like that. He knows all of my stories, she thinks. But he'll take them to his grave.

She thinks of the story she will tell Spoke, if she has the chance. If he doesn't go to his grave without it. Her story could be told in other people's things. The postcards and the photographs. A garnet ring and a needlepoint of the Homestead. The aprons hanging from her kitchen door. Her soft, faded and dog-eared copy of *The Little House in the Big Woods*. A closet full of dresses sewn before she was born.

All these things tell a story, but is it *hers*? It has always more than an aesthetic choice, holding onto the past, it is a kind of mourning. These things will not last.

We do not last, she thinks. In the end, only the stories survive.

She thinks of the photograph of the eleven-year-old girl, standing under a glacier, saying goodbye.

Then Michael says her name.

Isabel.

She holds her breath.

They are all quiet; their eyes rest on her. She doesn't know whether they are patiently attentive, or tired and needy, like children who will not fall asleep without one more story. She is the last. She thought that the party would be over by now. Wrung out. Everyone dreaming in their rumpled suits and dresses, piles of clothes in dozing heaps scattered over the furniture and floor.

Bell, Michael says again. Tell us a story—

She closes her eyes, but she can feel him looking at her, searching.

—about Longing, he says.

Oh, god she says under her breath.

She thinks of their first/last kiss, and the pang she felt, turning away from him. Spoke is already halfway across the country, where people are making breakfast, letting dogs out onto dewy lawns, boarding busses and trains for downtowns, lining up in coffee shops.

In Amsterdam, it is already a lovely afternoon, the leaves turning, fall about to break.

She opens her eyes. Through the tall windows, she sees a broken line of light between the buildings.

So she begins, I've never been to Amsterdam.